THIS IS NOT THE EXIT

Poems

Qiana Towns

Willow Books, a Division of Aquarius Press

Detroit, Michigan

THIS IS NOT THE EXIT

Editor: Randall Horton

Front cover photo by Thomas Sayers Ellis

Back cover photo by Adrienne Christian

Book design by Aquarius Press

Willow Books Emerging Poets & Writers Series

Willow Books, a Division of Aquarius Press
PO Box 23096
Detroit, MI 48223
www.WillowLit.net

Contents

The poem is an eye

    That ends and begins with a dream. Before

And after you've awakened

    It swallows you

Like a bite-sized Qi or a flower. It carries

    You through a head

With no absolutes, no efficacy. Dearest Reader,

    Why are you

Screaming when I haven't even cut you yet?

    Here you are dressed

For the party, draped in glory and me

    I am barely out of bed and halfway through

Another year of your life. Yes, you

    There with Occam's Razor at the back

Of your throat: another asteroid missed us—thank God?

    No, thank a poet or a poem.

Thank You.

VOYEURISM

> "Many […] live in a dream world of beautiful backgrounds.
> It wouldn't hurt them to get a taste of reality to wake them up."

I speak forcefully to the image: *If God is
a woman of her word, let me look once
and never again.*

Here in the safety of the future,
a woman's broken body. Her ruby
red nails and rouged lips hold

my eyes until I begin to chuckle
at her misfortune. It is a kind of laugh
reserved for awful instances—
broken falls, cries of desperation.

Were it not for her severed limb, snapped
and pointed straight toward heaven, one
might mistake her for an actress
penned between a dream and paycheck.

The caption says: Adela
Legaretta Rivas, struck by a Datsun
as she crossed Avenida Chapultepec. Even
as she lay dying or dead on a sidewalk, her beauty

transcends fortune. In the distance
a small sea of gawkers pause to stare
as if repulsion could save a life, then look
past Adela's body into oncoming history.

Whoever said the eye can see through
to the soul of man must not have
owned a camera. Whoever said man

cannot claim to have seen
a thing until it is photographed must
have been a disciple of Weegee.

If you arrive at my sickbed, confused
at the state of my body, remember this:
if I look alive, I must be
dead. The only way to keep me
here is to look.

The rulebook says not to care if they live or die.
If a woman screams dizzy loud enough her mind-well disengages.
If a man believes he is God then he is the founder of organized crime.
Religion is a jellyfish sting in the eye.
Only a prophet can count the ways to kill earth.
Setting fire to a bush is the same as going rogue.
A forefather once said the easiest thing about life is dying.
If a man runs the rat race on Easy Street it's a trap.
A black man, Chinese man, and John McCain go into a bar.
What he doesn't say is the answer.
The beloved disciple's lucky number is 13.
Seven miracles a day keep the oil from reaching.
The bottom of the ocean is still.
Anatomically, women need more hands.
Clapping may cause men to go blind.
5% of nail beds are made of fungi.
Swimming is a magic trick.

We dug cubbyholes in dirt mounds
left from expansion on the car plant
next to the tenement where
redlightgreenlight1-2-3 and down-
down-baby kept our bellies filled with laughs.

We constructed cardboard palaces complete
with hidden passages near the top of dirt
piles, laid our cribs out with shaggy rugs
and chiffon treatments hung to hide
squares cut for windows, spliced with filaments
from a stranger's garage.

And we I-spied the mamas tethered
to rotting wood porches talkin' 'bout
a white man makin' a movie about us, 'bout
how the company next door made off
with the life of our town, 'bout how they
didn't want no talk 'bout the white horse
destroying our community in the man's movie.

And we named ourselves Dirt Dobbles,
never intending to stay in the gutters
where we were born, never intending
to ride that white horse. Each day we watched
the car plant's entrance from our earth
houses, waited for the pity christ
to show up with a camera and a gaffer
boy to record the jagged edges
of our lives, make us as famous,
or at least offer a nickel for our troubles.

ACEY DUECEY

Fear has died a profane death. It looks
 like I'll be another year in America, chewing
my fingernails and waiting
for a newly seasoned America to show
up and freeze me
out from her bowels. Michigan is shitty
which is to say I am the proprietor
of nothing; not yet forty
and my joints ache even
after reefer. As a child my mother taught
me to play American Acey Duecey.
Or did my mother teach me
to roll a joint and all I remember
is her burnt ashes? I am shaking in boots,
hungry and without
loyalties. Americans are
so fucking greedy,
especially the 99% who drink
from my fingers. I raised
my hand in church to ask if
the ancient Californians had tongues.
The usher hit me with the collection plate.
I remastered My Country 'Tis
of Thee and now I want french fries. My first language
is Ebonics and America is a girl
my cousin took behind the pulpit
to do the oochie-coochie
during a Pagan Dance. And what? I am
the proprietor of even less than
I thought and, Ommerike, I want out
of this deal, yo. My daughter's a teenager
and she's into white boys.Go(o)ddamnit.
Off with this land. Trade
these blasphemous fragments for a narrow moon and never
show me an American son
again. I can't afford him anymore
than I can afford to be
without him. I hope you are

confused...maybe it was the Humpty Dance?
A year from now I am
on the midnight train to Jo-burg
to take my boo thing behind the pulpit. Call him
My Second Tongue.
When the conductor says
one-two-one-two
the people will shout *tjaila*. If
Michigan be an affricate or a fricative
dress his ass in an American flag
and fuck his short
and narrow channels, between the tongue
and avelora ridge. It's as high
as you'll ever be. Do it. Don't
be skurred.

Miss Sippy Rocks Steady on Montana Red's Birthday

Let his graphite stick
Swim laps in lean dark
Meeting places, on
Green double-damned blades
Of thick thread worn through.
Watch Cut-man's mean chops

Keep order with bug
Pussy traps, pistol
Just a crack away from
Dead. Eat Ida Mae's
Quarter chicken snaps.
On Montana Red's

Birthday they call for
A special lady
To dance a jig on
Him. With her wig dipped
To the right side, Miss
Sippy rocks steady

To the dance floor, them
Mens keep they eyes on.
The plywood floor aches,
Yearning to give way
Below Miss Sippy
The beats keep moving—

Folks upside the pool
Table dancing,
Eight ball grooves along.
But Miss Sippy want
Cash. *Go see him Miss
Sippy, roll them rich*

*Threads. Sharp! Miss Sippy,
Honey lose your soul
Throw it gone for bread.*

He got a muzzle
Like a trout. He want
To tie lips. *Keep on*

Twistin' Miss Sippy
Put him on his back.
Give him the eclipse
Let him know you is,
Miss Sippy let him
Breathe. One Miss Sippy.

Two Mississippi.
Them fancy threads, that
Cane River Creole
Magic keeps Miss Sippy
Pacifying Red,
Dancing the dollars home.

WAR RELICS

1.

In a house divided even the insects have to choose sides.
The roaches know three things:

One: The cast iron skillet's off limits.
Two: Women call out to God even when they're fucking angry.
Three: If the world enters the room, hide the children from light.

2.

In Korea, the messmen kept their dicks cupped
in their palms as they slept. They peeled back
the foreskin before dawn in anticipation.

3.

 In this house we tap out our secrets
on flesh.

One tap to the age line tells time of its wastings.
A fingernail to each palm means it is well.
Three fists to the gut mean infinity.

This is the sign language of sin;
this is how we figure the women.

Baltimore, After

i.
Eyes are hardest just after
a full day of rain. Today I made
myself a promise. My lashes
thin as bristles, I blink back
words. *I'll learn to speak more softly.*
Lucky you.

ii.
Today I've gone the distance
all the way over to sky
and beyond with words
to keep a circle from knowing
its name. No mas. Truth is I've grown
tired of being man. I miss the old animal me.

iii.
Aqueous humor:
my anterior and posterior have
ulterior motives, but let's not talk
with our lions full. Our passions flatten
rainforests so why should I look forward
to the new forward?

iv.
Longing is a puzzle's bloody uncle
so, if you've come here looking
for words to paint the language
of water don't expect to find a goddamn thing
to do with whatever you see.

v.
If this is your first time reading
a poem, allow me to re-introduce myself.

Westchester Lady

His *she* is only time, only
a blues string—never a note.
The poet and his odalisque
make moons when they touch.

The bodies are ovals;
the minds are vegetation.

The bodies are spinning.
The minds are agave.

Together they are incongruent.
So, the poet returns to the page,
no further from blues
than from the moonshine
in her cup, the moonlight at her flesh.

It has been a year and time is still
failing. In her dream his bare feet
tramp as they do in waking;

a dust storm whirls between
their bodies. She extends her arms,
offers her embrace to bind the living

with the already lived. He arrives
at the threshold only to turn back
to watch the birth of moons
or the passing of time, depending.

Ghazal

The pit bull rests on his side in the morning.
He waits for his pup to finish breakfast in the morning.

The three babies he has left bark at echoes,
pawing at their shadows in the morning.

Though your breasts are empty there is substance.
We are always paradoxical in the morning.

Remember? We watch the dogs from bed.
You pant like heat held your breath in the morning.

I massage your areola with my thumb,
tickle your nipples with my tongue in the morning.

As the sun walked in through the window,
you hide your breasts from light in the morning.

The care you took to conceal your shame is tragic.
We are finished making love in the morning.

Perhaps this is all visceral:
I am not in love, but I am hungry in the morning.

Desperately Seeking My Name is Not Susan

I've been meaning
to re-answer your ad
for love, Love.
> Another way to look at it is to taste it.
> Consume seven pineapples in a sitting
> and wait for the acid to take your tongue.

Truth is, I've had too many
beers to care about meaning, too much
red wine to know the difference
between man and sliver. Hell, I'm no Madonna.
> Look, all you really need
> to know is if Mississippi is the opening
> of a thousand drying river beds.

'Cause the sun's been promising
to return, and when it does
some woman in Michigan will shiver
and wait to feed you the blacks of her desperate eyes.
She is not me.
> When you are no longer here I will call out to whichever
> shadow I think is you. I will sing the lonesome
> girl's prayer with new lyrics. Say, we'll all be better off
> without you in the end.

Fish and Finger Snapping

I ask *Uncle, how you learn*
how to switch yo hips like a lady.
Because grandma said men walk
upright like Dr. King & Jesus.

>He say, *I was born a fish, a catfish*
>*with peppermint fins and a sweet tail.*
>   *When my mama found out she tried*
>   *to filet me but I wiggled from her grasp…*
>   *ended up in a stream where kids*
>   *let me sway as I please.*

Then his girlfriend, who was really a man
in a nappy blonde wig, halter top and tiara, snapped
her fingers and bent her lips like the matrix.
I didn't get it but the way they laughed
over the music and it was all right.

BEHEST OF A FADING DIVA
                    —for Uncle Vincent

Don't let nobody fuck with the guppies
or the lavender girls at drama club. Lonnie and Teeka
need dresses for ball, and somebody go with November
to get her test results when they come back.

Clear up the rumors behind me. Let them bitches
know I ain't gone crazy and I ain't on Jenny Crank.
I ain't killed no weenie dog, wrapped the bible in silk
with a hot glue gun or swallowed globs Vaseline.
I was shining my face, protecting my skin
from the wind.

This wheelchair is just cause I'm tired, you know.
I been stomping the catwalk with these feets
longer than these kids been alive. A bitch needs
rest and relaxation at the end of the day.

Don't let them hurt over me, lingering and snotting
like school girls recollecting old love.
It's like my big sister Carolyn used to say:
*Pain is real but it don't mean we need to feel it
everywhere we breathe.*

Tell them bitches I ain't dying,
I'm just looking for another place to live.

Ars Poetica

Sometimes me and poetry have to have it out. Poetry be like, "I need you to focus." I be like, "Don't you see I'm trying to watch Eat, Pray, Love again?" Poetry be like, "LISTEN, FISH STICK!" (Because in my head Poetry sounds like one of the 'kids.') And I be like, "You got it, P." And Poetry be like, "Naw! *hand gesture* Just gone!" And I be like, "Don't be waving your wordy hands in my face, dude." We carry on like this until...well, until I give up. Poetry wins every time. And my friend be like, "You know I don't pray, but I think you need prayer." And I be like, "Don't pray for me; pray for Poetry." And poetry be like...

FEAR OF A BLACK NAME

among the inner city walls
the only thing moving
is the eye of the girl with the black name

*

a girl and her mother
are one
a girl, her black name, and her mother
are one

*

I would have been Brandon [not a black name]
had it not been for Emilio Pucci

*

my black name is derived from fabric

*

the seams of my black
name are for worship

*

I wish for wishes, settle
for idiosyncratic scrapes in my black name

*

truth is difficult to bend
the fibers of my black name aren't as lucky

*

wash
my
black
name
in
a

fountain
with
pennies
for
luck

*

a black name is poetic invention

*

on land
my black name
runs from
suburbs
like fire ants

*

George and Georgina go to Georgia
Louis and Louise go to or St. Louis
Where do I go with my black name?

*

in Trout County
my black name means yankee

*

being born
in the year of the (black name) snake means
no sudden movement

*

1 year from now
new cave men will speak
my black name

*

and it has lived its own
life since

THE QIANA SHIRT, 1976, BY EMILIO PUCCI

1.
In her hair we see a psychedelic mantra
of a decade known as the We Speak
Bold-Faced Patterns epoch because names are
not unlike shirts we cover and press
the differences, a phonetic charade.
Watch how letters like collars precede
and manage dimensions, watch them march
into a history of preoccupation with self.

2.
The letter 'q' without 'u' is not unlike wolves& half-moons & coke spoons
& Rick James
& disco balls & Funky town & sex & healing & breath & thump, thump,
thump, thump.

3.
Skin is as wide as bishop sleeves
as consumerism:
A favorite summer fabric
pelted Stochastic Moniker red.

She wants to tell you
a story about the time
she bought her name in a city
where seams show through to bone.

Social Lithography or After Malaquis Montoya's "George Jackson Lives, Murdered in 1971 by San Quentin Guards"

sad how good it feels to see
the last of the world's black ink   paint

a mouth split   a body flood it
with golden syncopation   fingers

rest or slip
into assonance
same shameless   narrative

black bodies shackled
mouths bound with white
space for futures   histories

which tend to

make specimens of black
bodies   of shame

mountains of yellow and red and blue   blood
to ink new revolutions
to make less   dead

                                   the art of reform
                                   the truth of art

[The Last Supper-California]

> "We all have food in common."
> —Julie Green, painte

Plate 2   December 2005
Requested no last supper
Final meal: breakfast: oatmeal + white milk

Plate 7   May 1996
Pork chops + baked potato + asparagus + tossed salad + white milk
Mothers say it's the kind of meal that sticks to the ribs

Plate 12   May 1936
Death cell breakfast   Death
Painted in indigo against whiteness

Plate 3   January 2002/Plate 18   January 1930/Plate 19   January 1930
And for dessert: pie: Georgia peaches
Sweetness stored on the inside

Tonight after we have finished our last meal
Of the day each of us [being the artless beings
We are] will scrape meat and potatoes into the
Trash. Even after we have spent the day taking
Freedom for granted we will do nothing and be
Apathetic believing there will always be a next time.

There is snow white innocence
in the center of a mitten quiet
college town adjacent to the reservation.
The university has welcomed me,
neophyte blessed with an unfamiliar face.

When my jalopy becomes stymied
near a gas station on a dark road, I am
grateful for the police officer
who appears before the gas station patron,
dirty blonde and scruffy, can offer assistance.
His voyeuristic stare, like iced wind,

trails the policeman to my window.
The officer's smile chills at the sight of my hue.
He pantomimes words, pulls his flashlight
from his waist, rolls the light
over my back seat and into my eyes,
connotations of history.

He flashes light over the steering wheel,
an order to try the ignition When the car starts
his face says *save your breath*; light
over door handle says *get out*. Before
he can uncover a line for me to walk
the gas station patron arrival brings the officer's
face back to life. The small man pulls
at his skull cap he recalls watching my jalopy
roll into the lane and lose power.

I make circles in the snow with my heel,
brace for another round with Michigan's wind.

Acknowledgments

Thanks to the editors and staff of the following journals in whose pages these poems have appeared:

Crab Orchard Review ("Voyeurism"), *Poets for Living Waters* ("Big Blank Page for Marine Life"), *Tidal Basin Review* ("Social Regard"), *Pindeldyboz* ("Miss Sippy Rocks Steady on Montana Red's Birthday"), *No Tell Motel* ("War Relics" and "Westchester Lady" formally titled "Wholeman the DirtyHot Dream"), *thethepoetry* ("Desperately Seeking My Name is Not Susan"), *Reverie* ("Best of a Fading Diva" and "The Tension Between Black Girls and Cops is Not Imagined" formally titled "Extrapolation"), *The Rumpus* ("The Qiana Shirt, 1976, By Emilio Pucci"), *2ⁿᵈ and Church* ("600 Plates").

"Social Regard" was also published in *MidAmerica* as the 2014 winner of the Gwendolyn Brooks Poetry Prize.

The poet wishes to express gratitude to the Cave Canem Foundation, the Virginia Center for Creative Arts, and Bread Loaf Writer's Conference. These poems quite possibly would not exist without the support of these organizations.

The poet also wishes to thank Samaura, Cassidy, and all of the family members, teachers, friends and colleagues who contributed to this manuscript in one way or another.

About the Poet

Qiana Towns earned a MFA from Bowling Green State University, and a MA from Central Michigan University where she served as poetry editor for the online literary journal *Temenos*. Her work has appeared in *Tidal Basin* and *Milk Money*. She is a Cave Canem fellow and served as an editor for the journal *Reverie: Midwest African American Literature*. She was a featured performer at the Idlewild Poets & Writers Conference and also featured at Springfed Arts. She is a past winner of the Gwendolyn Brooks Poetry Prize, sponsored by the Society for the Study of Midwestern Literature (SSML).

www.ingramcontent.com/pod-product-compliance
Lightning Source LLC
Chambersburg PA
CBHW020536120726
47904CB00003B/1097